In memory of
Michael Keith Zollman.

— P. Z.

For Liz.

— F. I.

Text © 2022 Pam Zollman • Illustrations © 2022 Frances Ives • Published in 2022 by Eerdmans Books for Young Readers
an imprint of Wm. B. Eerdmans Publishing Co., Grand Rapids, Michigan • www.eerdmans.com/youngreaders
All rights reserved • Manufactured in the United States of America • ISBN 978-0-8028-5499-5

30 29 28 27 26 25 24 23 22   1 2 3 4 5 6 7 8 9

A catalog record of this book is available from the Library of Congress • Illustrations created with mixed media

A portion of the author's royalties will be donated to St. Jude Children's Research Hospital to continue research to end childhood cancer.

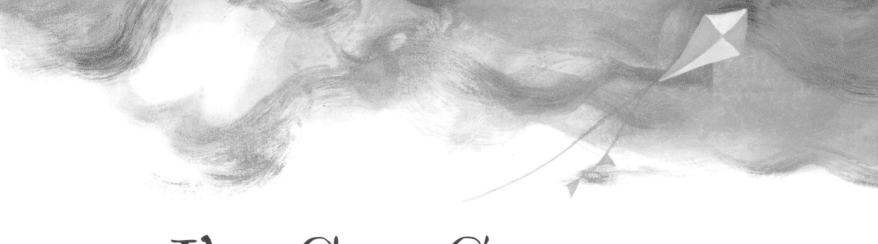

I'll Say Goodbye

PAM ZOLLMAN   FRANCES IVES

EERDMANS BOOKS FOR YOUNG READERS

GRAND RAPIDS, MICHIGAN

*T*he waves chase us, me and Uncle Mike.

We run in and out of the water, laughing and squealing. Then we collapse on the sand and breathe the salty air. Seagulls swarm the sky, crying for tidbits, scolding us for forgetting the bread crumbs.

I see a pretty shell by the water's edge, a gift from the ocean.
But when I reach for it, it moves!

Uncle Mike laughs and picks it up. "It's a hermit crab."

Inside the shell, a scary-looking creature peeks out, waving its antennae.

"Why is it in there?" I ask.

"That's its home." My uncle hands me the shell.

The crab squeezes inside the shell as I peer closer. It isn't scary, just scared. I decide to name it Herman and keep it as a pet.

"Someday Herman will outgrow this shell," Uncle Mike says, and helps me find a larger one.

A strong breeze ruffles my hair. Uncle Mike used to have dark hair like mine, but not anymore.

He has cancer, and the treatment the doctors use makes his hair fall out. So he wears a baseball cap all the time, even on the beach. He says a hat is a home for his head.

When he feels good, we spend all day by the water.
I like to fly kites, and Uncle Mike sits in the shade
and watches. He points out a sandpiper and warns
me to stay away from jellyfish.

The beach is where my uncle lives. He has a house on stilts, and you can see the ocean from almost every window. Mom and I are staying here so we can help him.

A fish tank is where Herman lives. He carries his house on his back,
and I wonder if he dreams of the ocean. My uncle helps me feed him.

The sky has turned gray with rain clouds, and Uncle Mike feels sick. He can't feed the seagulls or chase the waves. So I put Herman in his bedroom.

Uncle Mike and Herman stare out the window at the ocean.

When my uncle has to go back to the hospital, Mom spends all day, every day with him. One morning Dad takes me to see Uncle Mike. He looks pale in the metal bed.

I climb up beside him, and he smiles. "How's Herman?"

"He misses you. I do, too." I hand him a whelk shell. "I found this for you. You can hear the ocean."

Uncle Mike holds the shell to his ear. "I needed this." Then he lies back down.

Mom says we have to leave so my uncle can rest.

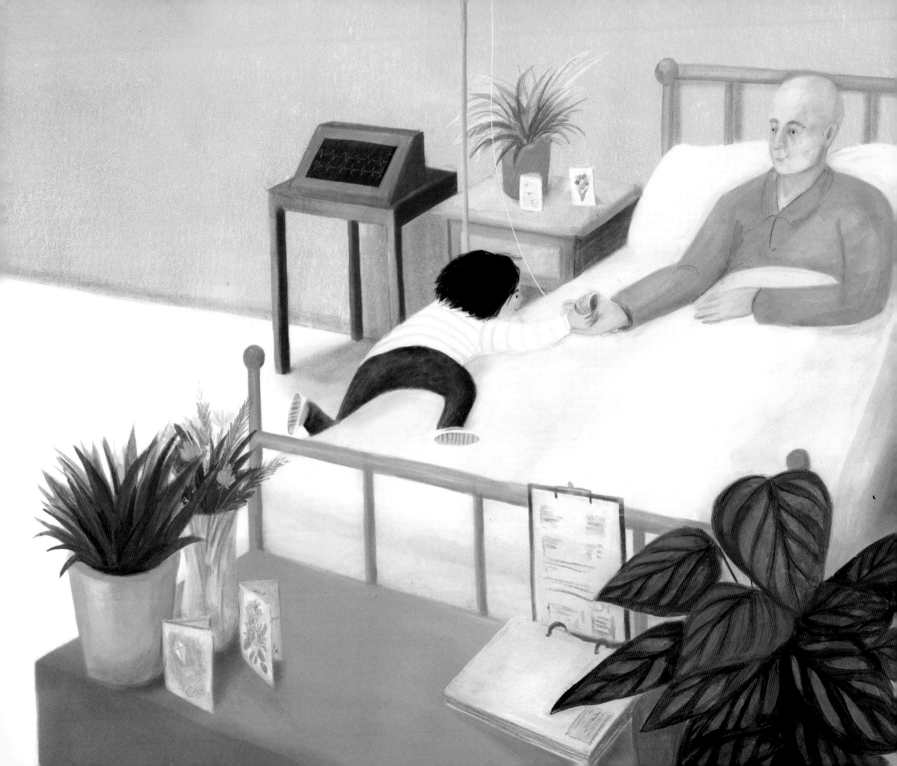

The beach isn't any fun without Uncle Mike. I wish he would hurry up and get better.

My grandparents come, but they don't come to see me. They spend all day at the hospital with Mom and Uncle Mike. And then they come home at night with sad faces. Sometimes I can hear them cry.

Every day I ask Dad when my uncle is coming home. Dad says he doesn't know, and he looks really unhappy when he says it.

I ask Dad about when I can visit Uncle Mike again, but he shakes his head. Dad tells me that my uncle is now in a special germ-free room, and the hospital says I'm too young to visit.

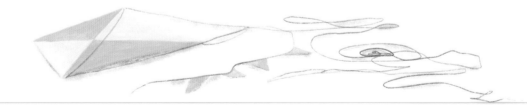

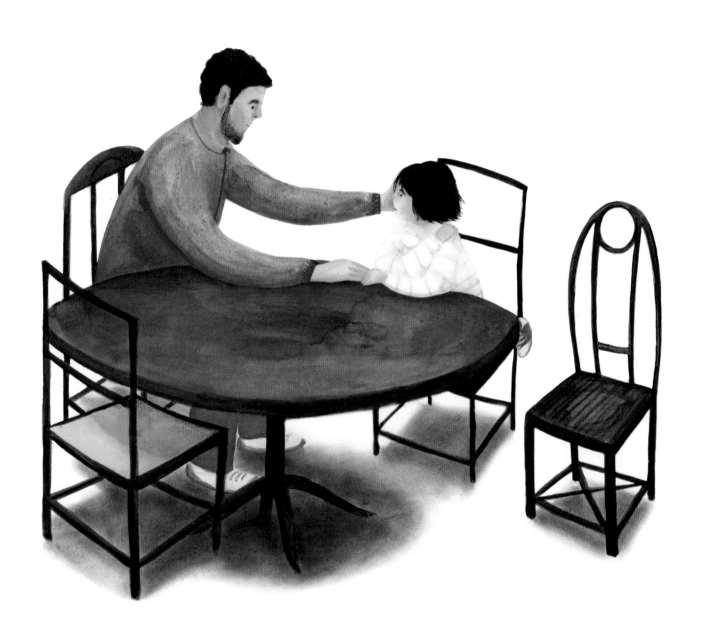

I go into Uncle Mike's bedroom and stare out the window with Herman. The ocean with its whitecaps looks upset, too.

And then everyone comes home from the hospital.

Everyone, except Uncle Mike.

My parents say that my uncle isn't coming home ever again. They say he's gone to a better place. But I know they're wrong. What place could be better than Uncle Mike's house on the beach?

It's not fair. I never got to say goodbye.

Later, after the funeral, we go back to Uncle Mike's house on the beach. Everyone is sad and telling stories about him, remembering things he used to say and do. There are so many people that I think Uncle Mike's house needs to be bigger.

While they talk, I go look for Herman.

Herman is still in my uncle's bedroom. His fish tank is still in the window, looking out at the ocean. But Herman is different.

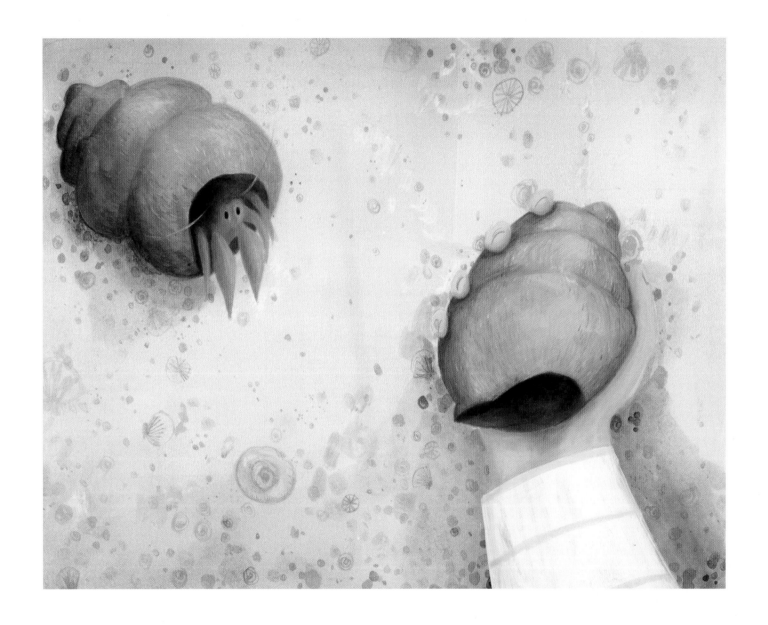

He has moved out of the smaller shell and into the larger one. The old shell is empty, no longer needed. I hold it in my hand.

Uncle Mike's baseball cap is lying on the dresser.
Closing my eyes, I press my face into its softness.

The cap still smells like him. I put it on my head.
It's too big, but I know I'll grow into it.

Mom comes into the room and puts her arms around me.
She hugs me tight.

"Uncle Mike really isn't coming back, is he?" I ask.

She doesn't speak, just shakes her head and wipes at her eyes
with a crumpled tissue.

I gaze out the window at the ocean. The waves look lonely.
"I'm going to miss him."

"Me too," Mom says as she hugs me again.

I take Herman out of his fish tank and go outside. The waves tug at my feet. Kneeling, I place Herman on the sand and watch him scurry toward the water.

"Goodbye, Herman," I say. Then I look down at the old shell in my hand and whisper, "Goodbye, Uncle Mike."